BEA... bananas

poems by
JoHN RICE

illustrated by
CHARLES FUGE

SIMON & SCHUSTER

LONDON • SYDNEY • NEW YORK • TOKYO • SINGAPORE • TORONTO

BEARS DON'T LIKE BANANAS

Monkeys like to play the drums,
    badgers wear bandanas.
Tigers like to tickle toes
    but bears don't like bananas.

A crocodile can juggle buns
    on visits to his Nana's.
Seagulls like to dance and sing
    but bears don't like bananas.

Rats and mice can somersault
    and do gymnastics with iguanas.
Weasels like to wiggle legs
    but bears don't like bananas.

A porcupine likes drinking tea,
    and cheering at gymkhanas.
A ladybird likes eating pies
    but bears don't like bananas.

ANIMAL ANIMANNERS

I don't suppose
a crocodile knows
about hygiene and washing his face.

I don't suppose
an elephant knows
about flying a rocket through space.

I couldn't care less
if a frog made a mess
and scattered his toys everywhere.

I couldn't care less
if a mouse changed his vest
and built a swimming pool under my chair.

It's nothing to me
to hear a sheep up a tree
singing a song about Sunday.

It's nothing to me
to spot a pig in the sea
swim all the way back to last Monday.

I don't give a hoot
if a bird in a boot
decided to take up farming.

But I do draw the line
when I watch a dinosaur dine,
that's something I find quite alarming.

BIRDWORD

If ravenous means I am hungry
    does swiftous mean fleet of foot?
would larkous mean I can sing well
    and owlous I don't give a hoot?

PARK POND

The park pond sparkles
    grey and white,
In places it is mucky.

The water isn't really
    deep, it's
just halfway up the ducky.

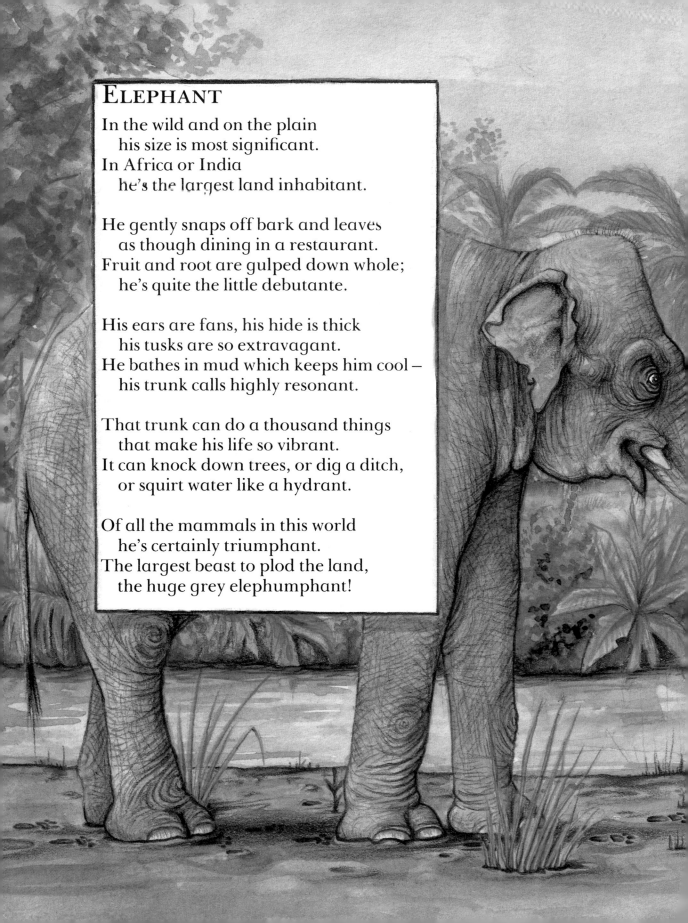

Elephant

In the wild and on the plain
    his size is most significant.
In Africa or India
    he's the largest land inhabitant.

He gently snaps off bark and leaves
    as though dining in a restaurant.
Fruit and root are gulped down whole;
    he's quite the little debutante.

His ears are fans, his hide is thick
    his tusks are so extravagant.
He bathes in mud which keeps him cool –
    his trunk calls highly resonant.

That trunk can do a thousand things
    that make his life so vibrant.
It can knock down trees, or dig a ditch,
    or squirt water like a hydrant.

Of all the mammals in this world
    he's certainly triumphant.
The largest beast to plod the land,
    the huge grey elephumphant!

TIGRESS

The Indian sun rises
and floods the swamp with light.

A tigress stretches
from a coiled rope to a straight sword.

She heads north to hunt.
Her back arches, her tail swings.

Her eyes are as clear as sunlight,
her stripes flow like water.

A stealthy, measured approach:
she focuses on her prey.

Final rush of air, bolt and strike!
Tigress, queen of hunters, brings drama to the day.

STRELKA

I am the star
that squints in the sky

I am the sky
that squats on the cloud

I am the cloud
that squirts the earth

I am the earth
that squeezes the worm

I am the worm
that squirms under the bird

I am the bird
that squawks at the cloud

I am the cloud
that squelches in the sky

I am the sky
that squabbles with stars

I am the star
that squints in the sky

SLEEPLESS NIGHT

I woke up at one
    the night had begun.

I woke up at two
    the moon in full view.

I woke up at three
    a whispering tree.

I woke up at four
    saw a shooting star soar.

I woke up at five
    when the birds come alive.

I woke up at six
    when the tom cats do tricks.

I woke up at seven
    saw the moonsun in heaven.

I woke up at eight
    I don't want to be late . . .
    for breakfast!

WOODJOORATHA

Woodjooratha play the fiddle than the flute?
Woodjooratha play the banjo than the lute?
  Woodjooratha dance a tango
  with a crazy mixed-up mango?
Oh woodjooratha play the fiddle than the flute?

Woodjooratha eat a pancake than a pea?
Woodjooratha eat a flapjack than a flea?
  Woodjooratha become thinner
  than eat a dinosaur's dinner?
Oh woodjooratha eat a pancake than a pea?

Woodjooratha have a toothache than a twitch?
Woodjooratha have a headache than an itch?
  Woodjooratha have your health
  than a rich man's wealth?
Oh woodjooratha have a toothache than a twitch?

Woodjooratha learn to skateboard than to cook?
Woodjooratha read a comic than a book?
  Woodjooratha fill your head
  with a bucketful of lead?
Oh woodjooratha learn to skateboard than to cook?

CLIP-CLOPPOSITE

In the playground opposite
you can skip, jump and hopposite.

Dive in the pool opposite
and your ears will go popposite.

In the shop opposite
you can buy a lollipopposite.

If you climb the hill opposite
you will come to the topposite.

Sit in the chair opposite
just lie down and flopposite.

Jelly on the floor opposite
clean it with a mopposite.

If a rich man was your opposite
would you like to do a swopposite?

IMPOSSIBLE JOURNEYS

I'll never walk the length of an African Plain,
nor cross the Alps in a super-fast train.

I'll never take a taxi to Timbuktu
nor sail in a yacht to Tokyo Zoo.

I'll never parachute to descend on Crawley
nor travel with precision in a supermarket trolley.

I'll never see the grass of savannah lands
nor the shimmering haze of the Kalahari sands.

I'll never ride a Greyhound through New York State
nor find the long-lost key to the Golden Gate.

I'll never board a jet to visit Hong Kong
nor take a slow boat to China to play ping pong.

I'll never make another journey, you can ask me why,
because I've been everywhere . . . except Paraguay!

THE FOOD THAT GETS STUCK IN THE PLUG OF THE SINK

A soggy tomato
   and yesterday's peas,
a dried up sultana,
   a lump of green cheese!

It's juicy, it's fruity,
   it's green and it's pink,
the food that gets stuck
   in the plug of the sink.

Tea bags and spinach,
   bananas and beans,
some pasta and peelings
   a pig's intestines.

It's juicy, it's fruity,
   it's green and it's pink,
the food that gets stuck
   in the plug of the sink.

Mushrooms and meatballs,
   a pineapple chunk,
a fried egg and gravy,
   a sausage that sunk!

It's juicy, it's fruity,
   it's green and it's pink,
the food that gets stuck
   in the plug of the sink.

SYMMETRY

In the distance,
high on the horizon's heat-haze,
the railway tracks marry
under a tiny telegraph pole
guard of honour.
      Symmetry of sight.

Across a summer valley
a child calls 'hello' in cat-cry voice.
A hollow echo returns the word
in kitten-cry voice.
      Symmetry of sound

Deep, deep in the unseen sky
soft galaxies twist, spiral, spin,
explode and expand
in a bubble universe
that mirrors another, another.
      Symmetry of space.

Triangles, squares, circles,
line delights, shapes delicious,
patterns that bring constancy
to the chaos of nature
and the uncertainty of man.
        Symmetry of science.

Verse, chorus, verse, chorus:
the song folds over itself
like a turned-back sheet on a bed.
The melody falls, rises, falls.
        Symmetry of song.

The telling of untold tales
between two friends.
The hidden unspoken sharing of ideas.
One with a secret to tell,
one with a secret to keep.
        Symmetry of secrets.

18

AUTUMN SONG

There's a chill in the air
that wasn't there
just over a month ago.

There's a dew on the grass
each morning I pass
the field where the stream runs slow.

People gathering hops
farmers harvesting crops,
the countryside all of a bustle.

The bonfires are burning
the tractors are churning
and at night the leaves eerily rustle.

Ripe apples are falling,
lonely church bells are calling,
over orchards they sullenly ring.

The summer plants wilt
and my bed gets a quilt:
how I wish I could sleep until Spring.

COUSINS

Every evening
when the dark creeps in
like a smothering black cape,
our little family
— Mum, Dad, Brother, Sister, Gogo the cat and me —
we get together to huddle and cuddle
and keep us each safe.

Every night
when the moon rises like a white saucer,
our little family
— Mum, Dad, Brother, Sister, Gogo the cat and me —
go to bed in our warm rooms.
We tuck each other in
and sleep safe in green dreams.

But in another land,
when the same dark creeps in,
a broken family in a wild wind
looks to the same moon, red and angry,
and each makes a wish,
— Mum, Dad, Brother, Sister, Asmara the stray dog —
all ask for food, for medicine, for peace, for rain.
Just these, only these, do our beautiful cousins ask for.

WHO'S THERE?

Who's there?
Who's that hiding behind the brown trees,
lurking among the green undergrowth of the woodland?
It's us – the Tree-Elves and the Moss-People
and we are watching you
breaking branches without permission.

Who's there?
Who's that gliding over the wet rocks,
dancing and splashing at the sea's edge?
It's us – the Rock Sirens and Mer-Men
and we are watching you
pouring poison in our watery home.

Who's there?
Who's that drifting through the sparkling mist,
flying across bright skies, bursting out of clouds?
It's us – the Alven, we who travel in bubbles of air
and we are watching you
filling our palace of sky with dust and dirt.

Who's there?
Who's that running over mountains,
wading through cold rivers, striding over forests?
It's us – the Kelpies and Glashans,
the powerful beasts of the wiser world
and we are watching you
wasting these waters and hurting this land.

THE PIG FAMILY

The Pig family snorkles, happy as can be
out for a stroll and afternoon tea.
    Trudge, trudge, trudge
    in the sludge, sludge, sludge.

Mother sow is wary, her eye on the litter
watches where they wander, she's a piggy-baby-sitter.
    Troop, troop, troop
    as they stoop, stoop, stoop.

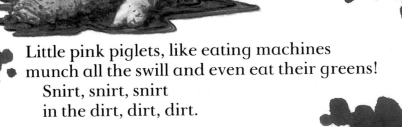

Little pink piglets, like eating machines
munch all the swill and even eat their greens!
    Snirt, snirt, snirt
    in the dirt, dirt, dirt.

Chubby little legs so deep in the muddle
they wear black wellies and paddle in the puddle.
Slurf, slurf, slurf
in the turf, turf, turf.

Small eyes like buttons to spot the pickings
pig-pink tongues to do all the lickings.
Clump, clump, clump
near the dump, dump, dump.

The Pig family chuckles, happy as can be
on the way home from afternoon tea.
Trudge, trudge, trudge
in the sludge, sludge, sludge.

SUNFIRE

"Who'll set me alight?"
said the wood one dark night,
"I'll have some fun,"
said the wakening sun.
"I'll set you on fire
as I climb higher and higher!"

"Who'll fan the flame?"
said the branch on its frame,
"I'll blow the trees,"
said the gathering breeze.
"I'll fan the fire
for my lungs never tire!"

"Who'll run from the blaze?"
said the deer in a daze,
"I'll warn the pack,"
said the fox at the back
"I'll raise the alarm
and we'll come to no harm."

"Who'll douse the embers?"
said the owl who remembers,
"I'll sting the glow,"
said the rain in its flow.
"I'll kill the flame
let me take the blame."

"Who'll grow us again?"
said the forest in pain,
"We'll take your seed,"
said the earth, stone and reed.
"We'll punish the sun
for the wrong he has done."

Look Up!

Look up!
The sky's a dark sea,
   still after a storm.

Look up!
The stars are fireflies,
   a still, unmoving swarm.

Look up!
The sun is playing hide-and-seek,
   still and quiet, but ever warm.

Look up!
The moon's a white eye,
   a still, unseeing form.

Look up!

LION

Who crowns you King of the Animals?
Who speaks of your arrogant stare?
And who admires your stealth?

Fast and fierce you are.

What long history can you tell of?
What future do you forsee?
And what power do you bring to the present?

Timeless and true you are.

RHINOCEROS

Like a huge mobile house
crossing the open plain,
the rhino heads for
the swampy banks of the brown river.

He washes, he drinks, he wallows.

Slabs of mud fall from his back
until his hide shows its true colour.

The rhinoceros turns
to search for shade.
He moves off,
  slow
    deliberate
      ponderous
– his hammer head lowered
in sad anguish.

MONKEY TRICKS OF NO MEAN ORDER

Deep in the jungle
where the sun never shines,
see the Mighty Monkey
swinging on the vines.

Deep in the jungle
climbing up the trees,
see the Mighty Monkey
bend her hairy knees.

Deep in the jungle
where the tall tree grows,
see the Mighty Monkey
scratch her coconut nose.

Deep in the jungle
hear the drums beat,
see the Mighty Monkey
shake her dancing feet.

Low Owl

Cold morn: on fork of two o'clock
owl's hoot flows from hood of wood.

Owl's song rolls from blood to brood,
owl's hoot loops on to top of town roofs,
owl's song swoops on strong doors.

Owl's slow whoop – long, forlorn –
soft flood of moon song.

Wolf World

Far from cities,
far from towns,
the wolf pack lives its solitary life.

Away from men,
away from change,
they have only the moon to colour them.

Afraid of the night,
scared of the dark,
humans hear only evil in the wolf's lonely call.

Ignorant of the future,
unwise about the past,
man must learn the ways and worldliness of the wolves.

POLAR BEAR

Padding through soft snow
the polar bears are pillows on a white sheet.

They are kings of their kind
roaming a majestic land of ice.

Who would want to destroy you,
ruler of this bright light wasteland?
Who does not hear your ancient song?
And who cannot see the dark
of this century in your great eyes?

Poems in this Book